Georgie and the Computer Bugs

Julia Jarman
and Damon Burnard

Happy zappy reading!

from Julia Jarman

Collins

Look out for more *Jets* from Collins

Jessy Runs Away • *Best Friends* • **Rachel Anderson**

Ivana the Inventor • *Ernest the Heroic Lion Tamer* • **Damon Burnard**

Two Hoots • *Almost Goodbye Guzzler* • **Helen Cresswell**

Shadows on the Barn • **Sara Garland**

Nora Bone • *The Mystery of Lydia Dustbin's Diamonds* • **Brough Girlin**

Thing on Two Legs • *Thing in a Box* • **Diana Hendry**

Desperate for a Dog • *More Dog Trouble* • **Rose Impey**

Georgie and the Dragon • *Georgie and the Planet Raider* • **Julia Jarma**

Free With Every Pack • **Robin Kingsland**

Mossop's Last Chance • *Mum's the Word* • **Michael Morpurgo**

Hiccup Harry • *Harry Moves House* • **Chris Powling**

Rattle and Hum, Robot Detectives • **Frank Rodgers**

Our Toilet's Haunted • **John Talbot**

Rhyming Russell • *Messages* • **Pat Thomson**

Monty the Dog Who Wears Glasses • *Monty's Ups and Downs* • **Colin We**

Ging Gang Goolie, it's an Alien • *Stone the Crows, it's a Vacuum Cleaner*
Bob Wilson

To Dai and Josie

First published by A & C Black Ltd in 1995
Published by Collins in 1995
13 12 11 10 9 8 7 6 5
Collins is an imprint of HarperCollins*Publishers*Ltd,
77–85 Fulham Palace Road, Hammersmith, London W6 8JB

The HarperCollins website address is
www.**fire**and**water**.com

ISBN 0 00 675005 2

Text © Julia Jarman 1995
Illustrations © Damon Burnard 1995

The author and the illustrator assert the moral right to be
identified as the author and the illustrator of the work.
A CIP record for this title is available from the British Library.
Printed and bound in Great Britain by
Clays Ltd, St Ives plc

Chapter One

Georgie Bell was off computers – right off. Weird things had been happening recently. She'd been sucked in twice! Yes, really! Into her computer! And she'd nearly been eaten by a dragon. Her brilliant brain had saved her – just – but she was definitely going to get a new hobby.

Yeah! Something safer...

... like bungy jumping!

She put a cloth over the computer.

What now?
It was while she was looking for something to do that she heard a voice.

At first she thought it was the Tank, her pestiferous little sister, but even the Tank – who could have spied for MI5 – couldn't get under that cloth. And that's where the voice was coming from.

It was a hoarse voice. Carefully
Georgie lifted the edge of the cloth.

Oh no! A dragon voice.
She dropped the cloth.
It was a hoarse dragon voice to be
precise, and Georgie knew exactly
which dragon it was.

Georgie covered her ears and
walked away. This was even weirder
than before. The computer wasn't
even plugged in!

Chapter Two

Georgie paced the room.

But it was too late. The Tank was already in.

Definitely too late – she was lifting the cloth.

The dragon was still begging for
help and his voice was weaker now.

Georgie looked.
The dragon looked terrible. His
nose was running and his fire had
gone out. His face was covered with
spots – purple spots with yellow
centres that *glowed* – and he was
shaking violently.

He moved aside to let Georgie see his children, huddled in a four-poster bed.

'Where are you?' said Georgie.
'I don't know,' said the dragon.
'I've taken a room in some ancient hostelry. We were on our way home when the bugs struck.'
Only then did Georgie notice the disc in the disc drive.

'Poor Daphne. Poor Dennis. Poor Deidre,' said the Tank. All three were covered with spots that glowed, and their teeth were chattering.

The dragon did look ill, but Georgie still didn't trust him. It might be a trick.

The dragon waved weakly at the window. 'Look at all those graves,' he said.

'Because it's a *computer* virus, G . . . e . . . orgie, and you're the computer ace – aren't you? There are bugs in the system.' This last speech exhausted him and he collapsed beside the bed.

Chapter Three

Georgie
thought
about it.

Bugs in the system were quite
common and sometimes the cure
was easy. You just switched off and
they disappeared. She'd try that –
and switch off the dragon at the
same time!

Warily – she didn't want to get too
close – she reached out and
switched OFF,
with the tip
of her finger.

Nothing happened! The dragon was
still there and so were his children.

She peered behind the computer. It still wasn't plugged in, so what was going on? And where were those bugs?

Georgie still suspected foul play, but she could see something in the corner of the screen.

It was an evil-looking creature with four eyes. Sparks zig-zagged off its wiry feelers.

It's...it's like the butcher's electric fly-catcher!

She was right. Something went too close . . .

. . . and it was gone.

Electric! Of course! Georgie's brain worked fast. The bugs were electric, generating their own electricity.

So that's why the computer didn't need to be plugged in!

There are lots of bugs, Georgie!

The Tank was pointing at them. Georgie pulled her away.

Careful, Tank! Get back!

There was a row of dirty white ones on the edge of the pillow behind the young dragons' heads.

There were clusters of yellow ones on the bed curtains. Every now and again one of them flashed.

'See,' the dragon's voice was faint.

Georgie did see – and it made her even more determined to stay out of it.

Chapter Four

The Tank was determined to stay.

Fortunately, Georgie managed to drag Tank on to the landing. Unfortunately, she tripped over the cat, and Tank shot back into the room.

Georgie shot after her.

But Tank's finger was already on
the ENTER key and . . .

. . . the computer was roaring like a
hungry hoover.

Georgie dived for the Tank's legs
but . . .

. . . it was too late.

Georgie pounded the RETURN key.
She pounded the EXIT key. She
held it down. She prayed. And the
spinning screen went into reverse.

There was a flash like lightning, and out of the screen crawled . . .

Georgie squished it . . .

. . . but another appeared . . .

. . . and another!

Then the face of an enormous bug
filled the screen.

Its voice sizzled with satisfaction.

'Sssss. . .uper Bug at your service,
Ma'am.' The creature bowed, and a
red something on the top of its head
wobbled.

'We're taking over, you ss. . .ee.'
It sizzled again. 'We've sss. . .tarted,
and s. . .so we'll finish. Ha!'
Suddenly Georgie remembered Tank.
Where was she?
Any moment now her mother would
be calling them for dinner.

'We're so powerful, Georgie. We've wiped out whole programmes. We've ruined banks.'

we've brought down GOVERNMENTS!

It was true. Georgie had read about it in the papers.
But – Georgie cheered up – she'd read about something else too.
She remembered an advertisement in *Computer Weekly*:

CLASSIFIED
BUGS IN THE SYSTEM?
use our ANTI-VIRUS TOOL KIT!
Results guaranteed!
Allow seven days for delivery

She had to think of a plan, fast.
More bugs were tumbling out of the
disc drive . . .

. . . dropping on to the keyboard . . .

. . . and rolling on to the floor.

Chapter Five

Georgie ran to the bathroom.
It would have to be DIY.

In seconds she was back with the
bottle. Bugs were germs, weren't
they?
Georgie squirted furiously at the
bugs near her feet.

'It won't work, Georgie,' Super Bug was *laughing*.

The bugs vanished beneath the spray, but they soon reappeared. Georgie squirted again.
But the bugs fought back, and as the bottle ran dry they emerged from the foam, shaking themselves like small wet dogs.

'HA! HA! HA! HA! HA! HA! ' Super Bug was having convulsions of laughter.

Super Bug was exultant. 'That label says "Kills all KNOWN germs", Georgie, but . . .' he was laughing so much he could hardly talk.

Georgie raised her foot, but as she brought it down . . .

. . . the bugs rose in a swarm, then hung from the lampshade.

Time was running out.

She studied the keyboard.
DELETE? She might delete Tank.
SEARCH? That was better. She
must find the Tank.
Above her the bugs hummed.

Georgie didn't like leaving them on the
loose, but she hadn't much choice.

She pressed SEARCH, and a
mountainous terrain appeared.

She pressed again. This time she
got the dragon's lair.

The door was open but there was no
sign of the dragons. No sign of the
Tank either.
She pressed
SEARCH again.

This looked more promising.
A village appeared. It seemed to be
deserted, but she thought she
recognised the ancient hostelry.

Were the dragons in there?
Was the Tank?
Georgie knew she'd have to go in.
A cabbagey smell was climbing the
stairs.

Her mother would be close behind.

Chapter Six

Quickly she flicked through the menus.

Another menu came up.

An idea was beginning to come to her. She really needed more time to think, but her mother was in an impatient mood.

'No ifs, Georgie! If you're not down in ten seconds flat there'll be trouble!' she yelled.

Georgie plugged in her computer.

She reckoned that if she did defeat the bugs – and she had to – she would need an electricity supply to get out again.

Then Georgie pressed ENTER.

But by the time Mrs Bell entered
Georgie's bedroom . . .

. . . Georgie had gone.

Chapter Seven

VROOSH!

Through the computer screen
and aeons of time into . . .

. . . a medieval village
where Super Bug
and his troops were
waiting.

Battle was about to begin.
Score so far:

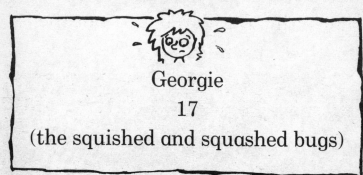

Georgie
17
(the squished and squashed bugs)

Bugs
1,999,993
(their victims)

Fortunately, the bugs didn't see
Georgie arrive because Mrs Bell had
plunged the scene into darkness
while trying to turn off the
computer.

Unfortunately, Georgie couldn't see much either – only from time to time a tiny flashing light – but the torch was useful.

The bugs made a noise like the hum of a fridge. Georgie looked all around.

On three sides were cottages and on the other a church. Here and there a spotty body slumped against a wall.

She could just make out a notice saying BRING OUT YOUR DEAD. It was leaning against a cart piled high with bodies – all of them covered with the dreaded purple and yellow spots.

In the graveyard was a sign saying
FULL.

There were crosses on many of the
cottage doors and on the door of *Ye
Travellers (Last) Rest.*

There was a dim light in an upstairs window. Georgie decided she must go in.

Two voices answered her from different directions.

said one voice.

said the other.

Georgie followed the first voice and found herself in a cowshed facing a cow's bottom.

said the cow.

screamed a milkmaid.

And Georgie had a BRILLIANT
thought.

What had happened was this:

1. The milkmaid saw Georgie and screamed.

She had never seen a twentieth century person before and thought Georgie was a ghost or evil spirit.

2. The cow, hearing the milkmaid scream, kicked the bucket – which hit Georgie's leg, at the same time as milk from its udders squirted into her eye.

3. Georgie turned to look at the milkmaid and was amazed by what she saw.

And the cow MOO-ed.

And this led to Georgie's great discovery. Call it déjà vu, or déjà moo or even déjà poo (for the cow's breath was disgusting), whatever, Georgie had the answer – *im-moo-nisation*!

At that moment she heard the Tank's voice from upstairs.

Georgie knew what she had to do.

Chapter Eight

It was hard getting the cow upstairs, but as she pulled and sometimes pushed, Georgie had an inspiring thought. She would take her place among those famous men and women who had pushed back the frontiers of science and saved the world from life-threatening diseases.

At last Georgie and the cow reached
the top.

And there was the Tank, looking
every bit a Florence Nightingale,
tending the dragons, though she
herself didn't look well.

Georgie signalled to her to keep
quiet, but it was too late. The bugs
had heard everything. And they
hadn't been idle.

Already the score was:

Georgie	Bugs
17	1,999,994

Their latest victim was the village bell-ringer. He'd been hanging on, but the battle for life had finally become too much for him.

As he let go of the rope, the bell tolled and Super Bug gave the signal to attack . . .

. . . and the bugs descended.

Fortunately, the cow,
who couldn't stand the
sound of bells, moo-ed
mournfully.

MOO and bugs met head on.

The moo was quite powerful.
A few bugs fell to the ground.

After the first round the score was:

Georgie 169	Bugs 1,999,994

Super Bug ordered the bugs to re-group.
They did – into two swarms.

ATTACK!

After Round Two the score was:

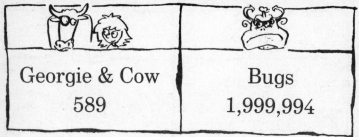

Georgie & Cow 589	Bugs 1,999,994

Super Bug grew angry.

YOU CALL THAT AN ATTACK?

YOU SHOULD BE ASHAMED OF YOURSELVES!

He ordered the bugs to attack properly, and this time they did. Unfortunately, the cow was eating some leaves growing through the window. Georgie couldn't persuade her to leave them.

For several minutes the bugs did
their worst. They stung, sizzled
and bit.

The Tank swatted, splatted and
stamped, and actually managed to
squish a few.
Georgie urged the cow to moo but it
went on chomping the leaves.

From his vantage point on the headboard, Super Bug crackled hysterically. 'Ha ha HA! Any second now, Georgie Bell, you'll be covered with spots!'

But no spots appeared on Georgie. She didn't feel terrible. She felt quite well. So did the Tank! Immoonisation was working!

The score was now:

Georgie & Cow & Tank 1012	Bugs 1,999,994

Super Bug grew furious.

Georgie explained to the Tank about immoonisation. 'If the cow doesn't moo we can't fight back,' said Georgie, 'and she's clearly not in the mood.'

The Tank pulled the cow's tail –
and the cow was not pleased.
Her moos filled the room.
The noise was terrible.

The smell was worse, but the effect
was miraculous. As Georgie and the
Tank watched, the dragons' spots
started to fade.

The bedposts rattled. The walls shook and in ones and twos, and then in dozens, the bugs started to fall to the floor with their legs in the air – waving.

Then the waving seemed slower.

And so was Super Bug!

All of them vanished. (Well, all except one in Georgie's bedroom.)

The score was now:

 Georgie & Cow 1,999,999	Bugs 1,999,994

Georgie could hardly believe it. Nor could the dragon. Hoarse no longer, he was talking to his children.

Chapter Nine

What happened next is a bit of a
mystery. Mrs Bell was in a very bad
mood.

Suddenly, seeing what she thought
was a fly on the computer – it was
the last bug – she bashed it . . .

. . . and accidentally pressed the EXIT
key . . .

Seconds later, Mrs Bell found herself
flat on her back.